Building My Self-eSTEAM in Science

Activity Book

Who are scientists?

By Yasmine Daniels, PhD

ISBN 979-8-9858843-0-2.

Printed in the United States of America.

Published by M.O.M. Successfully, LLC.

Edited by Kendy Gustave.

Illustrated by Saher Nazir.

Acknowledgements are extended to McBride Collection of Stories and HH Pax for their initial contributions to Building My Self-eSTEAM in Science volume 1.

Note to Parents

Dear Parents,

By now you may have already read my first book, **Building My Self-eSTEAM in Science volume 1**, which teaches youth about the importance of friendship and confidence through an education in science, technology, engineering, art and mathematics (STEAM).

As your little one grows, it is important to continue to remind them that science is all around us. This book is designed to help children answer the question, "**Who are scientists?**" and to engage them in a series of fun, science-themed activities while doing so. It will help them to see that a scientist can be anyone - even one of them! Remember, it's never too early to get children excited about science, technology, engineering, art and mathematics (STEAM).

Dr. Yasmine Daniels

Table of Contents

Instructions

There are ten (10) activities within this book, which are designed to go along with the story portrayed in the book **Building My Self-eSTEAM in Science volume 1**. The activities within this book will help to answer the question, "**Who are scientists?**" and they will encourage us to think about science from a few different perspectives.

As each exercise is completed, take some time to color the characters and scenes on the adjacent pages which go along with each activity. Be creative and have fun!

At the end of the book, be sure to check your answers using the provided **Answer Key** and to fill out your **Certificate of Completion**. You may choose to detach your certificate and hang it up or frame it.

Activity 1

What does a scientist look like?

Draw a picture of what you think a scientist looks like.

Where have you seen a scientist before?

Answer: _______________________________________

(3)

Do scientists work in teams?
Color!
page
ELITE
SCIENCE
4

Activity 2
Lost Scientist in a Maze

Can you help this scientist find her science team?

Start

Finish

Fun
Fact

Groups of scientists come together all the time to work on experiments and projects. This is usually called a collaboration.

Do scientists work in a lab?
Coloring page
6

Activity 3
Lab Word Search

Try to find the hidden words for things found in a lab.

K E E T V E P O C S O R C I M
S S R C E Q R C E E F J A U H
A Q A U H O D V H L U K Y H L
M X W L P E O T M G N L A A R
P F S X F L M G K G N D I S H
L V S Q G I R I A O E V P C M
E G A U U R L V C G L J N V X
P G L L H C S N W A E B V A D
H Z G P M Y U K K O L L I Q C
B W T L R U D R D A B A B Y V
D H X I L A B C O A T F E V X
O L N S D F K M F G I U A Y Y
Y G E P N Q F G P R M B K M K
E Z K T S I T N E I C S E C Z
I C S F H G A J H Y N U R M A

beaker	chemical	dish
fire	flask	funnel
glassware	gloves	goggles
labcoat	microscope	sample
scientist	syringe	vial

Fun Fact

In a lab, a scientist may carry out a number of experiments using chemicals, glassware, instruments and personal protective equipment (PPE) like gloves and goggles.

Can scientists be bakers?
Color! page
BAKING POWDER
FLOUR
8

Activity 4
Cake Science Matching

Match each ingredient (or reactant) listed on the left with its purpose on the right. Each ingredient is part of the recipe for baking a cake (or product).

Ingredients

flour

butter

sugar

water

eggs

baking powder

Purpose

used to help combine and dissolve all ingredients

forms the cake's main structure and contains gluten

a source of fat that makes the cake creamy and fluffy

makes the cake sweet, soft and moist

helps the cake rise

keeps the cake's ingredients together and acts like an emulsifier

Fun Fact

Many of the ingredients used to bake a cake go through a chemical reaction when the cake batter is placed into the oven.

Do scientists use math?
Color-page
10

Activity 5
Lab on a Budget

Decide which item(s) you can afford to buy for your lab using a $10 budget then add them to your shopping bag(s) below.

Fun Fact: Scientists use numbers and math for many reasons, especially to measure and count things in the lab.

Do scientists like sports?
Color! page
12

Activity 6
The Science of Bones

Can you name these human bones?

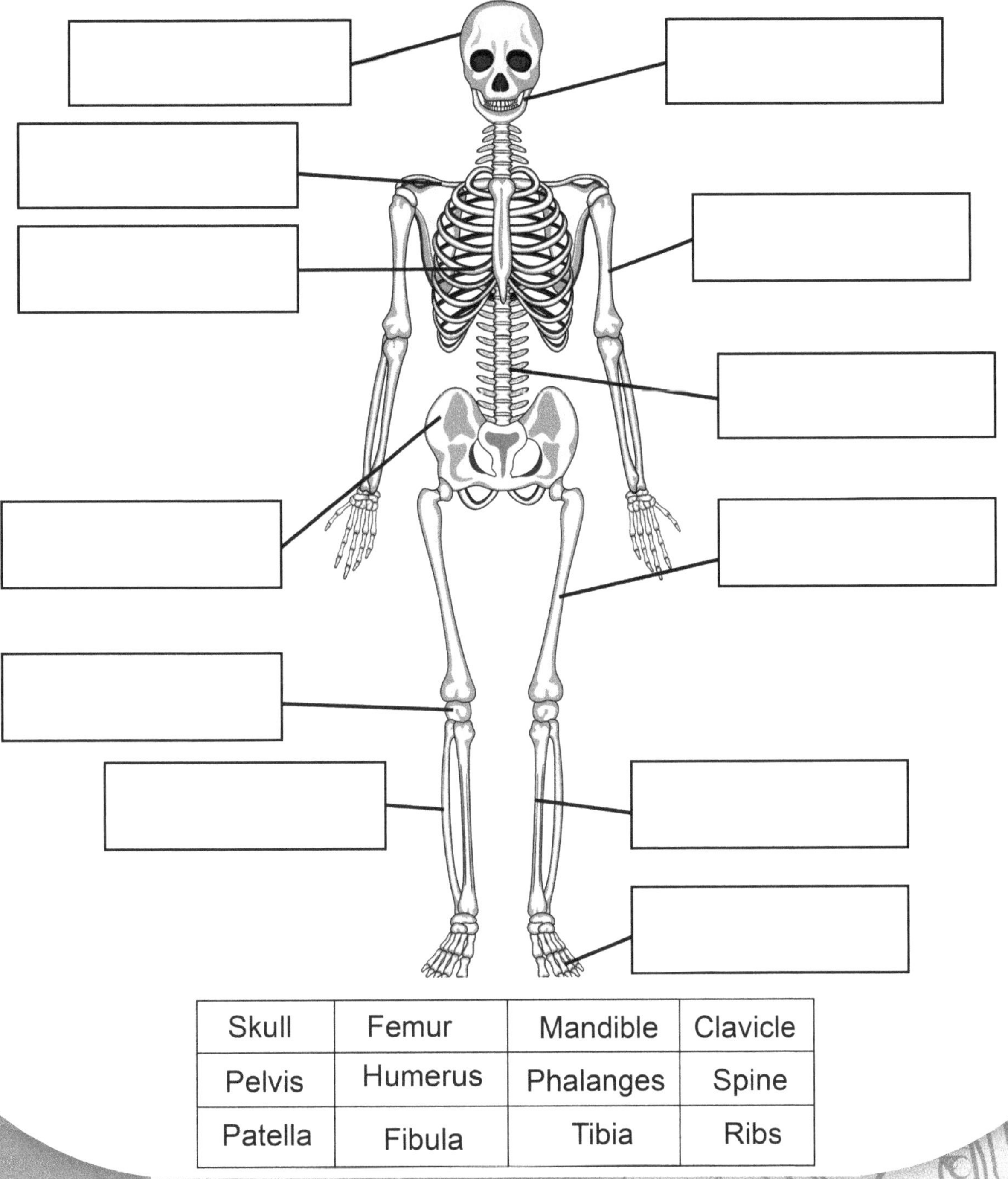

Skull	Femur	Mandible	Clavicle
Pelvis	Humerus	Phalanges	Spine
Patella	Fibula	Tibia	Ribs

Fun Fact

Scientists who study the way the body moves are called Kinesiologists.

Can scientists make cars work?
Color!
page
P
14

Activity 7
Science and Cars Crossword Puzzle

Use the clues below to find the missing science words related to cars.

ACROSS

3. cleans dirt and oil
4. liquid used to wash a car
6. it makes the car do work
8. keeps the engine in good shape
9. how fast something goes

DOWN

1. fuel for a car
2. you can change the color of a car using this
5. material that tires are made of
7. the powerhouse of the car

Fun Fact: Gasoline is a chemical that is used in most cars to make them work. It is made of a mixture of many different hydrogen- and carbon-containing compounds called hydrocarbons.

Do scientists like to dance?
Coloring page
HAPPY BIRTHDAY

Activity 8
Rhythm and Patterns

Can you match these science words with the non-science words that they rhyme with? One has already been done for you.

Beaker   Road

Explode   Cube

Microscope   Taxi cab

Experiment   Speaker

Lab   Basement

Test tube   Jump rope

Fun Fact: Music is made up of sound waves that scientists have shown travel through air, liquids and solids.

Can scientists be investigators?

Activity 9
Science Investigator Word Scramble

How good are you at investigating? Try unscrambling these words, which are related to a forensic science investigation.

SYRMEYT

NICEDEVE — 5

VESOL — 2

ESCA — 8

NAD

ERBPO — 3

NIDTFIEY

TPSUSEC — 1, 6

OISUCPSSUI — 7

ERCMI — 4

TLIAR

ESITSNW

CENSE

AWELYR

OOLDB

1	2	3	4	5	6	7	8

Can a scientist look like me?
Color!! page
20

Activity 10
My Science Story

Fill in the blanks to tell your own, unique science story.

I like science because it is ______________________.
Whenever I see something new, I like to ask
__________________________. No question is ever
stupid or silly. My favorite science experiment is the
__________________.

When I am doing science, it makes me feel
____________________. Science helps me understand
how ______________________ works. My favorite place
to do science is at the __________________. Whenever I
go there I always like to look at the
__________________. As a scientist, I write things down
in my ________________. I like working with other
scientists because they are ________________________.

One day I will become a ___________________________
scientist and I will invent a
__________________________________.

Answer Key

The answers to some activities have been provided below.

Activity 3

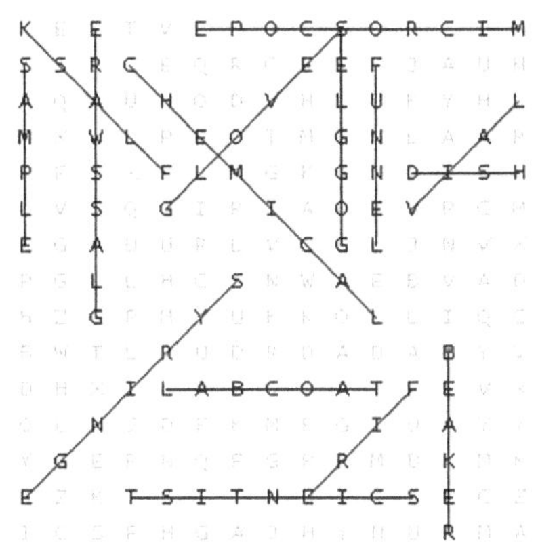

Activity 4

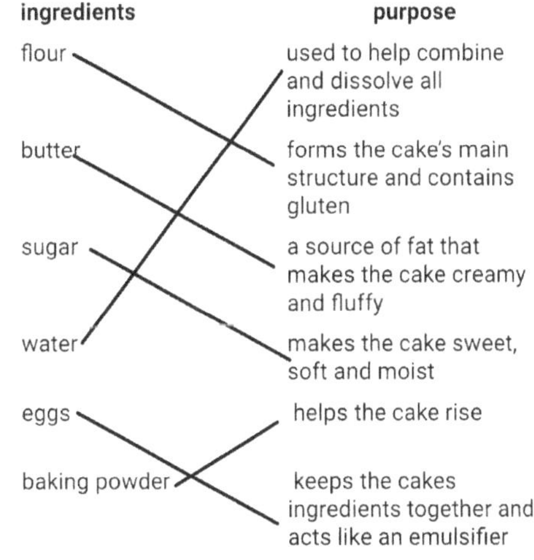

Activity 6

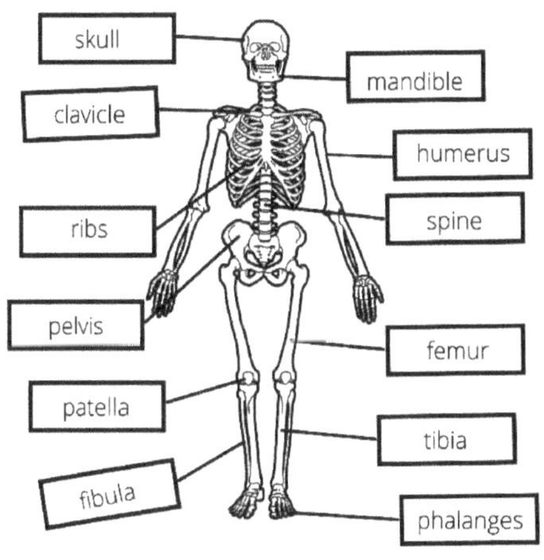

Activity 7

Activity 8

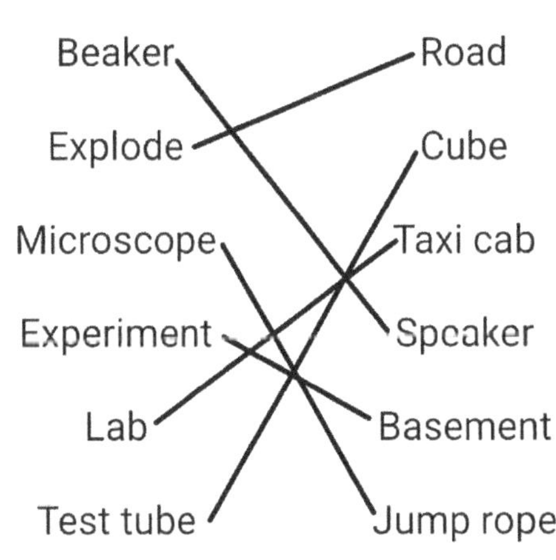

Activity 9

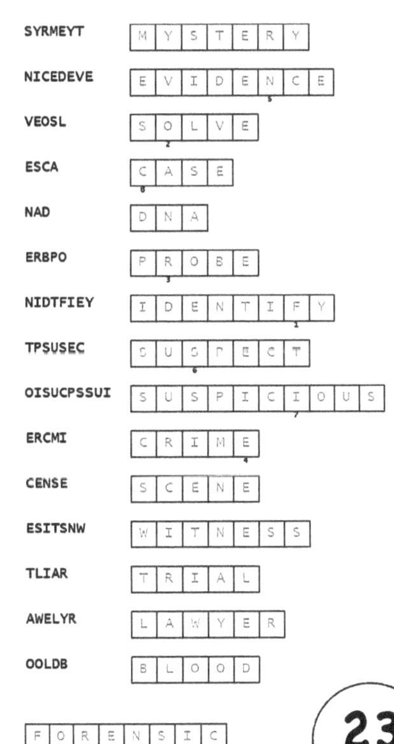

Visit www.classychemist.com for more.

Certificate of Completion

This is granted to

For Being an Outstanding Scientist

Yasmine Daniels

Dr. Yasmine Daniels
Author, Chemist, Mentor